What Emily Saw

Written & Illustrated by
Kathryn Otoshi

"Good morning, Emily!"

What's this under here? Is it a party for me?

MAX

Oh, I see. The mice just got married!

Look over here, Max! Are the pirates on the run?

AMANDA
P.G.W.
Heather
S.GILLINGHAM
THE ART OF Robert MacKenzie
HAWKINS
Brice Cox
JS
J.SCHINDEL
W.FU
Otoshi Family
Blue Ink
M. RUSSELL
MSI
SCEVOLA
Daniel Jeannette
STEVE JONES
MSI
E. DILLINGER
G. MORRIS
Horizon
ELLISON
Bromley
Frank Lee
D.CHIANG

They've popped the cork and are headed straight for the sun!

Let's go outside, Max. It's a beautiful day!

Look! A tornado of butterflies coming our way!

Bringing men with balloons having afternoon tea.

Now why is this mountain moving underneath me?
Hello, Mrs. Dino. How do you do?

Let's play hide-and-seek all afternoon.

Found you! Goodbye, Mrs. Dino.
Come visit me soon!

Look, Max, a key! Does it open that gate?

We'll go inside where a kingdom awaits…

...home!

"Goodnight, Emily.
Sweet dreams, Little Love."

Look, Max! See that star shooting up in the sky?
We can chase it to the moon when we close our eyes

KATHRYN OTOSHI *is an illustrator and writer living in the Bay Area. What Emily Saw is her first independently published book under* KO KIDS BOOKS. *She is currently working on her next two children's books, Simon & the Sock Monster and the Gargoyle de St. Belle.*

Thanks to Mike Scevola at MSI Litho, Publishers Group West, and H & Y Printing for their professionalism, dedication, and support. Special thanks to Daniel Jeannette for his advice and belief in this book.

KO KIDS BOOKS *is dedicated to creating fine quality children's books. The inside of this book is typeset in Mrs. Eaves on matte paper using a 4-color process.*

Please visit us at www.kokidsbooks.com